God Gave Us the World

by Lisa Tawn Bergren   •   art by Laura J. Bryant

GOD GAVE US THE WORLD
PUBLISHED BY WATERBROOK PRESS
12265 Oracle Boulevard, Suite 200
Colorado Springs, Colorado 80921

ISBN 978-1-4000-7448-8

Published in the United States by WaterBrook Multnomah, an imprint of the Crown Publishing Group, a division of Random House Inc., New York.

WATERBROOK and its deer colophon are registered trademarks of Random House Inc.

Library of Congress Cataloging-in-Publication Data
Bergren, Lisa Tawn.
    God gave us the world / by Lisa Tawn Bergren ; [illustrations by Laura J. Bryant]—1st ed.
        p. cm.
    Summary: While visiting a museum, Mama Bear tells Little Cub about all the different kinds of bears living around the world, and that God created this big, diverse planet to be their home.
    ISBN 978-1-4000-7448-8
    [1. Creation—Fiction. 2. Christian life—Fiction. 3. Polar bear—Fiction. 4. Bears—Fiction.]
I. Bryant, Laura J., ill. II. Title.
    PZ7.B452233Gor 2011
    [E]—dc22
                                        2010011910

Printed in the United States of America
2011—First Edition

10 9 8 7 6 5 4 3 2 1

*For Jack, may you know how wide
and wonderful God's world really is…*

"What a beautiful world we live in!" Mama Bear said. "Just look at all this snow!"

Little Cub looked around. "We *always* have snow, Mama."

"Yes, but it's *always* different! Sometimes it's slushy, and
sometimes dry, shimmering sparkles drifting from the sky.
But this is my favorite kind of snow...big, fat flakes you
can catch with your tongue!"

Little Cub giggled when she saw Mama
trying to catch flakes on her tongue.
"You look funny."

Mama smiled and nudged her with
her hip. "You do too. I think you
have the *pinkest* polar bear tongue
I've *ever* seen."

"Ever?"

"Ever."

"Do all bears have pink tongues?"

"I don't know, Little Cub. God made a whole world full of bears. And we all look a little different."

"He did? Why'd he do that?"

"Because God is creative. Just like he made all kinds of places to live, he made all kinds of different bears… and all kinds of different bear tongues."

"Whoa, whoa, whoa!" Little Cub said.
"There are other kinds of places to *live*?"

"Well sure," Mama said.
"While the Pole is our home, lots
of bears live in far different places."

"Why would they wanna do that?"

BEAR
EXHIBIT

"Because they like their homes best. It's where God put them.
God gave us this great big, wide world and a whole bunch of
different bears with different fur and different families."

"Where do those other bears live? I've never seen 'em!"

"All around the world, Little Cub. Some very far from here."

"Panda bears live in China.
All they eat is bamboo."

"What's bamboo?"

"A kind of tree."

"They eat trees for *breakfast*?"

"Breakfast, lunch, and dinner!"

SLOTH BEARS

"And there are sloth bears in India.
They hang from trees and like to eat termites."

"Bugs? Eew!"

"They think they're delicious. And they have the
longest tongues you've ever seen!" Mama said.

GRIZZLY
BEARS

"Here we are. Grizzly bears live in America.
They like to catch fish."

"Phew!" Little Cub said. "Finally another bear who eats
normal food."

Mama smiled. "Even though other bears eat what you
might not like, we're all bears. God made us all.
God made the world and everything in it."

"Why not make us all the same?"

"We're not all the same on the inside, are we?

Some of us are quiet,

others LOUD!

Some of us like to move *fast*,

and others take their **t-i-m-e**.

I think it's fun that God made us
all bears, but all special too."

"Don't those other bears miss snow?" Little Cub asked.

"Do you miss the sand of the desert? Or the big green leaves of the rain forest? We love what we know, because it's *home* to us. Every bear has a special place in God's great, big world."

"Why not put us *all* here? Why not make us *all* polar bears?"

"Oh, there wouldn't be room here for all of us! And the world reflects God's work. How big, big, BIG he is. God can do *anything.* And if he's capable of anything, why would he make us *all* polar bears?"

"The whole world is like a mirror of God's work, Little Cub. Out of all the places he could've put us, he chose this world, Earth, to be our home. He made it just for us. God gave us this special world and every creature in it."

"Why'd he do that? Put us on
Earth, I mean."

"Because he is the Creator.
Can you imagine your Grandma
not cooking something new?
Or your Grampa not working on
a new birdhouse in his shop?

God created our world and everything in it, because it's in his nature to create. Understanding that is part of why he put us here…to serve and worship him, our amazing God, who gave us this amazing world."

"Do you 'member when he created it?"

Mama laughed. "Our world is older than anyone can remember. It's older than my great-grandmother's great-grandmother."

"Whoa, that's old. Like that huge ol' tree in the forest?"

"Older."

"It must be very strong."

"Very strong. And yet fragile too. We have to take care of our world. It's God's gift to us. He'd be sad if we hurt it."

"God might get mad if we hurt our world," Little Cub said.
"I get mad when the twins hurt my stuff."

"Yes, I understand that," Mama said, picking her up.
"We don't want to make God mad or sad. We want him
to smile. We want to take care of this world he gave us."

"Do you think we'll ever meet the other bears?"

"Hmm. Maybe someday. It's a big world and constantly changing. It'd be fun to know more bears, wouldn't it?"

"Maybe a panda bear will come on an iceberg and bring us some bamboo!"

Mama laughed. "It's always good to make new friends, try new things, and know more about this world that God gave us."

Little Cub went to sleep that night, thinking about the stars in the sky and her special world.

She thought of other little bears falling to sleep, in forests and caves and jungles. And she was glad that God had made her, little her, to be one of the bears in it.

Also Available:

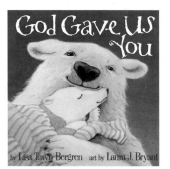
ISBN: 978-1-57856-323-4

ISBN: 978-1-57856-507-8

ISBN: 978-1-4000-7175-3

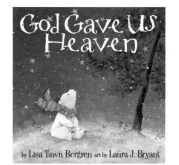
ISBN: 978-1-4000-7446-4

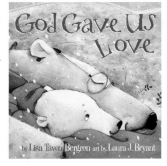
ISBN: 978-1-4000-7447-1

Over one million copies in the series sold!